Look Out!

Written by Barrie Wade
Illustrated by Tim Archbold

Collins Educational
An imprint of HarperCollins*Publishers*

Look out! There's a mad monster behind you!
Oh no there isn't!

Oh yes there is!

Look out! There's a dreadful dragon behind you!
Oh no there isn't!

Oh yes there is!

Look out!
There's a greedy ghost
behind you!
Oh no there isn't!

Oh yes there is!

Look out!